THAT APPLE IS MINE!

RETOLD AND ILLUSTRATED BY KATYA ARNOLD

HOLIDAY HOUSE · NEW YORK

Acknowledgments

Thanks to Sam Swope and Jon Agee for their support and valuable advice. Thanks also to Yvette Lenhart, my tasteful and patient designer. Last but not least, thanks to Noel Giddings for helping me develop a new sense of style and illustration.

Author's Note

Vladimir Suteev was a highly successful twentieth-century writer, artist, movie director, and producer. He was born in 1903 and became a kind of Russian Walt Disney. His films are sweet, funny, and full of action-packed adventure. Suteev was also famous for his many picture books, some originals and others based on his films. This dual talent for writing and drawing might be explained by the fact that Suteev wrote with his left hand and drew with his right!

That Apple Is Mine! is based on one of Suteev's stories. The text has been somewhat altered, but the mood and the meaning remain the same.

The illustrations for *That Apple Is Mine!* were completed in several steps. First, I created black line drawings, which were then reproduced on clear acetate sheets. Finally, I placed the sheets over collages I made from hand-painted papers glued on hand-painted backgrounds.

Copyright © 2000 by Katya Arnold
All Rights Reserved
Printed in the United States of America
www.holidayhouse.com
First Edition

Library of Congress Cataloging-in-Publication Data

Arnold, Katya
That apple is mine! /retold and illustrated by Katya Arnold; based on a story by V. Suteev. —1st ed.
p. cm.

Summary: In this retelling of a Russian folk tale, Rabbit, Crow, and Hedgehog fight over ownership of an apple, until Bear persuades them to share.

ISBN 0–8234–1629–1

[1. Folklore—Russia] I. Suteev, V. (Vladimir) II. Title.

PZ8.1.A7295 Th 2000
398.2'0947'0452—dc21
[E]   00-026797

Design: Yvette Lenhart

Hare said,
"Crow, pick
that apple for
me, please!"

Crow thought,
That apple looks good!
I want it!

So she picked the
apple off the tree
and flew away.

But the apple
was so heavy
that she

dropped it.

The apple landed right
on Hedgehog!
What a nice surprise!
he thought, and ran away.

"Hey, wait!" cried Hare.
"That apple is mine!"

Crow cried,
"No, that apple is mine!
I picked it."

Hedgehog cried,
"No, that apple is mine!
I caught it!"

Then Hare cried,
"No, that apple is mine!
I saw it first!"

Crow pecked Hedgehog on the snout. Hedgehog pricked Hare on the leg. And Hare yanked Crow's feathers.

They screamed and shouted so much they woke up Bear.

"What's going on?"

asked Bear.

"Crow stole **my** apple!"
said Hare.

"No!" said Crow. "That apple
is mine! Hedgehog
stole it from **me**!"

"I did not!" said Hedgehog.
"That apple is **mine**!"

Bear asked, **"Who saw the apple first?"** "Me!" said Hare.

"Who picked it?" "Me!" said Crow.

"Who caught it?" "Me!" squeaked Hedgehog.

"Then each of you deserves the apple," Bear said.

"But there's only one apple!" cried Hare, Crow, and Hedgehog.

"Well," Bear said,

"let's divide it evenly so each of you gets a piece."

They all agreed this was a wonderful idea. And Hedgehog cut the apple.

Hedgehog gave
the first piece to
Hare because Hare
saw the apple.

He gave the second
piece to Crow
because Crow
picked the apple.

He gave the third piece to himself because he caught the apple.

There was one piece left.

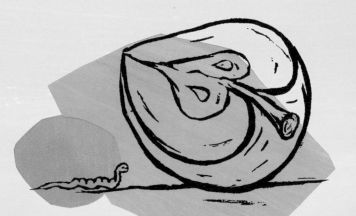

"Who's this piece for?"
asked Bear.

"You!" said Hedgehog.

"Because you stopped us from fighting."

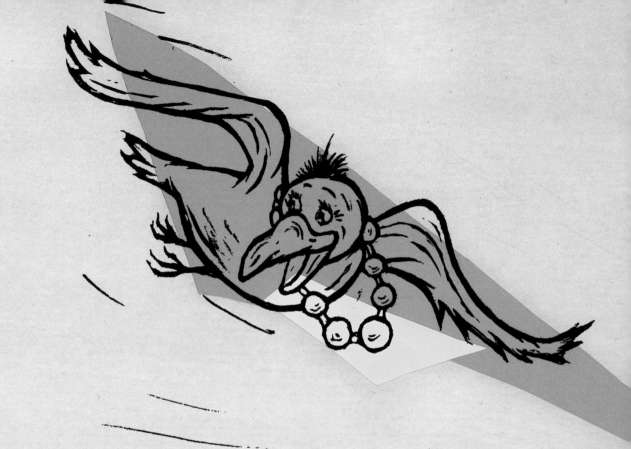

"Thank you, Bear,"
the animals said.

They ate up the apple.
And everyone was happy!

"But that apple was mine!"

said Worm.

And she crawled away to find another one.